RAINBOW
STREET
SHELTER

MISSING!
A Cat Called Buster

MISSING!
A Cat Called Buster

by Wendy Orr

illustrations by Susan Boase

Henry Holt and Company · New York

Henry Holt and Company, LLC
Publishers since 1866
175 Fifth Avenue
New York, NY 10010
mackids.com

Library of Congress Cataloging-in-Publication Data
Orr, Wendy.
Missing! A cat called Buster / Wendy Orr ; illustrations by Susan Boase.
— 1st ed.
p. cm. — (Rainbow Street Shelter ; 2)
Summary: After his pet rabbit dies, Josh feels sad and is determined not to own another pet until an elderly neighbor's cat goes missing.
[1. Cats—Fiction. 2. Pets—Fiction. 3. Lost and found possessions—Fiction. 4. Loss (Psychology)—Fiction.] I. Boase, Susan, ill. II. Title.
PZ7.O746Mi 2011 [Fic]—dc22 2010044786

ISBN 978-0-8050-8932-5 (HC)
1 3 5 7 9 10 8 6 4 2

ISBN 978-0-8050-9382-7 (PB)
1 3 5 7 9 10 8 6 4 2

First Edition—2011 / Book designed by April Ward
Printed in the United States of America by
R. R. Donnelley & Sons Company, Crawfordsville, Indiana

0811

For BC, Ginger, and Sally,
with special thanks to Buster, Muti,
Maisie, and Aacky-Magaacky
(and the people who live with them)

—W. O.

Buster and his sisters and brother were born in a box at the back of a garage. The three sisters were fluffy and pretty, and the brother was sleek and black.

Buster had a square head and a crooked white snip on his nose. His fur was as orange as marmalade on warm toast.

Their mother licked them clean, fed them, and looked after them so well that their cardboard box was as good a home as the comfiest cat basket. The kittens learned to open their eyes and look all around. They learned to wash their faces and paws clean with their scratchy tongues. And the mother cat kept them secret and safe.

One day, when the kittens were just old enough to walk and tumble and play, the mother cat led them out of the box to explore the world beyond the garage.

But as each tiny kitten came blinking out into its first bright sunlight, a hand grabbed it and dumped it into a sack. The

mother cat yowled and the kittens meowed, but the sack was dropped into a car and the mother cat was left behind.

The car drove down a long road while

the frightened kittens squirmed in the dark, squeezy sack. Then they felt a *whoosh!* as the sack was tossed from the car and a *thump!* as they landed on the grass beside the road.

No one saw it happen, and so no one ever knew who had done such a cruel and terrible thing.

Buster knew, but he couldn't say—except that for the rest of his life he hated purple baseball caps, going in cars, and being anywhere squeezy where he couldn't get out.

Luckily, the next person who drove down the road that day was a very different sort of person—and even more luckily, she saw the squirming sack. She didn't know what it was, but if it was squirming it must be alive, and if it was alive it didn't belong in a sack on the side of the road. Even though the bag squirmed so much that she was afraid it might be a snake, she stopped her car and walked slowly back while she tried to figure out what to do.

As she got closer, she heard a chorus of meowing.

The woman sprinted to the sack and ripped it open. She was furious at who-ever had dumped the kittens, sad for how scared they were, and so happy that she had found them. She wanted to take them all home and give them enough love and kindness that they would never be frightened again.

But she knew that one kitten was enough for her tiny apartment, so in the end she drove straight to the Rainbow Street Animal Shelter.

2

Rainbow Street was short and narrow. At the end, in the middle of a big garden with shady trees and green lawns, was a pale blue building. A seven-colored rainbow arched right across the front, with a cheery, cherry-red door in the middle.

Inside there was a gray parrot named

Gulliver who asked, “Can I help you?” in an old man’s gravelly voice, and a young woman with long dark hair wound up above a kind face and a name tag that said MONA.

The woman who’d rescued the kittens told Mona the story. She was still angry and sad as she described finding the bag on the side of the road.

“Of course we’ll look after the kittens!” Mona said, and went out to the car with the woman.

The woman picked up Buster’s brother. “This is the one I’m keeping.”

Mona reached in to gather up the other kittens. Three pretty, fluffy gray kittens meowed and snuggled into her arms. The orange kitten with the square head scratched and leapt out of the car.

Mona put the other kittens down again and raced after Buster. “Here, kitty, kitty!” she called.

The woman who’d found them raced after her. “Here, kitty, kitty!”

Buster didn’t listen. He raced down Rainbow Street and across someone’s front lawn. A big dog roared at him from behind a fence, and Buster streaked up the nearest tree.

It was a huge old oak tree, the tallest tree on the block.

Mona and the other woman looked up,

and up. “Meow,” they heard, from high in the tree.

Mona began to climb. She’d been rescuing animals since she was eight years old, and sometimes climbing trees was the only way to do it. She scrambled up to Buster’s branch and coaxed and murmured till he wiggled close enough that she could grab him and take him safely down.

The man in the house behind the oak tree took a picture of Mona rescuing the kitten and sent it to the newspaper.

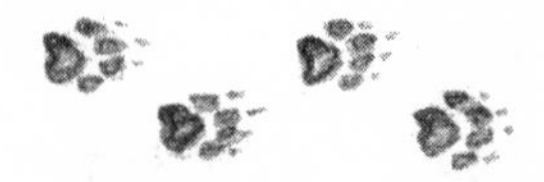

People who wanted a cat came to the Rainbow Street Animal Shelter to see the feisty orange kitten they had read about in

the newspaper, but when they got there, they saw Buster's pretty, fluffy sisters. "What adorable kittens!" they always said. And one after the other, Buster's three sisters went home with new families.

Buster was still not pretty or fluffy. He got taller and more orange every week, and he preferred to get to know people before he decided if he liked them. He liked Mona and Juan, the old man who volunteered at the shelter, but he wasn't sure about anyone else.

And he'd added big barking dogs to the list of things he didn't like.

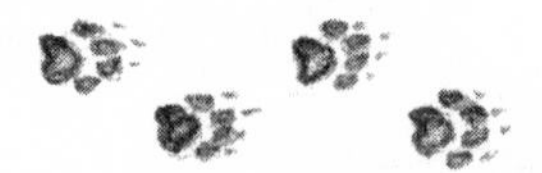

A few months later, when Buster was a

yowly, prowly, tall and rangy teenage orange kitten, a family took him home. Buster wouldn't sit on their laps, and he wouldn't stop chasing their dog—so after three days they took him back to Rainbow Street.

"Sorry, Buster," said Mona. "Maybe you'd better stay here and live with us, like Gulliver."

But deep inside, Mona kept on hoping that Buster would find his very own home. "The right people must be somewhere!" she said to Juan.

Finally, the right person came.

Mr. Larsen was very old, and he didn't want a brand-new, fluffy kitten.

"I don't care what color it is or what it

looks like," he said. "But I'll know when I meet the cat who's right for me."

Then he saw Buster lying in the sun on the roof of his cat kennel. Buster looked back at Mr. Larsen for a long minute. He jumped down, arched his back and stretched, then stalked over to meet the old man.

“A marmalade cat!” said Mr. Larsen. “I’ve always wanted a marmalade cat!”

“Buster hasn’t had an easy life,” said Mona. “He’s got a bit of an attitude.”

“I knew he was the cat for me!” said Mr. Larsen.

3

Just like Mr. Larsen knew that Buster was exactly the right cat for him, Josh knew that Rex was exactly the right bunny for him.

Rex was a big rabbit with soft, deep, orange fur. When he was younger, he used to like playing with a little red ball and exploring new parts of the garden. Once he'd even chased a stray cat out of the yard. Even when he was old, he sometimes felt so good that he did crazy bunny binky dances, with Josh and his sister, Mai, copying him, jumping and twisting around the floor. And when he was tired he liked lying on his back and having his tummy stroked till he went to sleep.

If Josh was sad, he always started to feel better again when the bunny sat on his lap and let Josh stroke him from behind his twitchy ears right down to his tail. Sometimes Josh thought there was some magic in Rex's soft fur that made bad things seem not so terrible.

Rex wasn't just Josh's rabbit; Mrs. Lee had him before she even met Mr. Lee. Then they got married, and then Mai was born, and then Josh, and then Rex was everyone's pet.

He had his own hutch to sleep in. For nice days he had a cage in the backyard that Josh and Mai moved around so he always had a fresh patch of grass to nibble. On cold rainy days he stayed inside and lolloped around the family room and kitchen. When he was inside he had a litter tray in the bathroom, and he never had an accident. (Except for the time he ate the cable to the computer modem and the time he ate the cell phone charger cord, but those were a different kind of accident.

“Bunnies make mistakes like everyone else,” said Josh’s mom.)

Rex never made those sorts of mistakes anymore. In the last few months, Rex had changed. He still liked to have his tummy stroked and tickled, but he lolloped so slowly it was barely a bounce, and he never did his binky dances anymore. He didn't do anything much except sleep and nibble.

But he was part of the Lees' family, and Josh loved him.

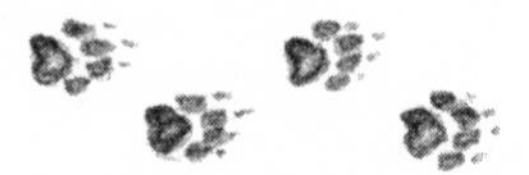

Buster was still young. He was two years old, and he'd lived with Mr. Larsen for more than half his life. He'd never stopped hating purple baseball caps, cars, squeezy places, and big dogs, but he'd found lots more things that he loved.

He liked going for walks, even though Mr. Larsen made him wear a harness and a leash. He liked lying in the sun and sitting on the porch beside Mr. Larsen. He liked chasing the carrot peels when Mr.

Larsen dropped them on the floor while he was making dinner. Most of all, he loved Mr. Larsen.

And Mr. Larsen thought he was the most perfect cat in the whole world.

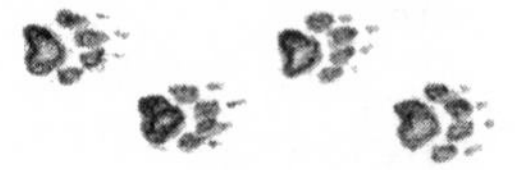

The first time Josh saw Buster, the cat and a very tall, very old man were walking home from the beach.

It was not a cute and fluffy kitty cat. It was the biggest cat Josh had ever seen—and people who didn't like cats might have even said it was ugly. It had a square head, a crooked white snip on its nose, and one bent-over ear that looked as if someone had taken a nibble out of the tip.

But it was exactly the same orange marmalade color as Rex, and Josh thought that was the most perfect color an animal friend could be.

It was also the only cat he'd ever seen walking on a leash.

"I'd never catch him if I let him loose," said the old man. "He chases every dog he sees, right down the beach and back again. Dogs don't know what to do when they see Buster coming!"

Josh didn't see the cat again for a long time, but he liked to think about him. There was something wild and crazy about a giant cat that chased dogs, as if he didn't even know that he was a cat.

Sometimes Josh felt wild and crazy, but he didn't know if he was brave. He knew for sure he wasn't big.

Josh's dad was tall and strong. His big sister, Mai, looked like their dad. But Josh's mom was short and skinny—and Josh looked like their mom.

4

This year Mai was going to middle school and Josh was going to walk to school by himself.

The Lees' house was on Spray Street. If you walked straight down their street for two blocks, then turned right for one block, you ended up at the Ocean Street corner where the schoolyard started. That was the way Mai always went.

Josh liked to turn right at the first corner to get to Ocean Street, then walk two blocks down it to get to the school. It was exactly the same distance and took him exactly the same time.

And it took him past the house where the very old man and the very large cat lived. Every morning as he walked to school, he saw them sitting outside on the porch in the sun.

The old man looked even older. Josh never saw him walking to the beach anymore, but he always waved as Josh walked by, and Josh waved back. The big cat sat

beside him, watching everything and every-one, as if he was deciding whether or not they needed to be chased away.

Josh liked the way Buster sat there on

guard beside his man. He thought he'd like having a pet who looked out for him like that—but then he felt mean, as if Rex might know what he was thinking, so the next day he walked the other way to school.

The day after that everything changed.

Rex had had a very long life for a bunny.

He'd had a very happy life too.

But Rex had lived as long as a rabbit can possibly live, and he was so very, very old that when he went to sleep that night, snuggled up safe in his hutch, he never woke up again.

Josh felt as if part of his life had been ripped away. And it didn't matter how much everyone said what a happy life he'd had or that it was Rex's time to go; the whole family was sad, and nothing seemed right.

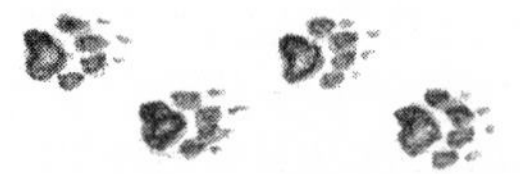

"It's hard to believe right now," said Mr. Lee, "but one day we'll be ready to get another pet."

"Maybe a dog that we could take for walks on the beach, " said Mai.

"Or another baby bunny," said Mrs. Lee. "You kids can't imagine how sweet Rex was when he was tiny."

"I don't ever want another pet!" Josh shouted. "I just want Rex!"

"We all do," said his mom.

"There'll never be another Rex," said his dad. "But when we're ready to have another pet, we'll learn to love it too."

Josh knew he'd never be ready. He didn't want to get used to another pet—and he never wanted to feel this sad again. It wasn't worth loving anything if it made you feel this bad when it died.

Now Josh didn't want to meet anyone with a pet. He walked the other way to school so that he didn't have to see Mr. Larsen and Buster. And he definitely didn't want to go to the First Monday of the Month Assembly. That was when Hannah stood up in front of the whole school to do a presentation about a pet who needed a home. Josh didn't know how she could do it; he didn't even like standing up in front of everyone in his class!

Josh had known Hannah since second grade. The two main things about Hannah were that she loved dogs and had a long ponytail that always told how she was feeling.

On the first day of school this year, her ponytail bounced with excitement when Hannah told the class about the dog she'd found, and then it moped sadly down her back when she said her parents had made her take the dog to the Rainbow Street Animal Shelter.

No one saw what the ponytail did next,

because the new boy, Logan, jumped out of his chair so fast he'd knocked his desk over. "His name is Bear!" he'd shouted. "He's my dog!"

So Logan had gotten his lost dog back, and Hannah had become a volunteer at the shelter. Even though she had her own dog now, she still went to Rainbow Street every week to help look after the lost animals. She helped feed the pets, clean out their cages, and play with them so they remembered how to trust people and be happy. And once a month, she told the school about a pet who needed a home.

Next Monday was the first Monday of the month.

Josh knew for sure that hearing sad

stories about lost animals wasn't going to make him feel any better at all.

Maybe I'll catch a cold and be too sick to go to school, Josh thought. He started practicing coughing just in case.

6

It was the scariest night of Buster's life. It was scarier than being dumped out of a car, being chased by big dogs, or being stuck at the top of a tall tree.

It started just like every other night. Mr. Larsen and Buster sat out on the porch after dinner till it was dark, then went inside and watched TV till bedtime.

TV-watching was the only time Buster sat on Mr. Larsen's lap. His purr started off as a whispery hum, but as the old man's hands stroked the thick fur from the top of his head, down his back to the start of his tail, Buster's purr rumbled louder and louder. After a few minutes, his whole body thrummed and he sounded like a fishing boat heading out to sea.

At bedtime, as Buster twined lovingly around his legs, Mr. Larsen made himself a mug of tea and poured a bit of milk into Buster's saucer. A splash of milk slopped onto the floor.

"That was a close one, Buster!" Mr. Larsen said.

"Meow," agreed Buster.

The old man turned to put the saucer down. He slipped in the spilled milk and crashed to the floor.

Buster meowed and prowled around him, but Mr. Larsen didn't move.

Buster didn't care about the spilled milk or the smashed saucer;
he just wanted his man

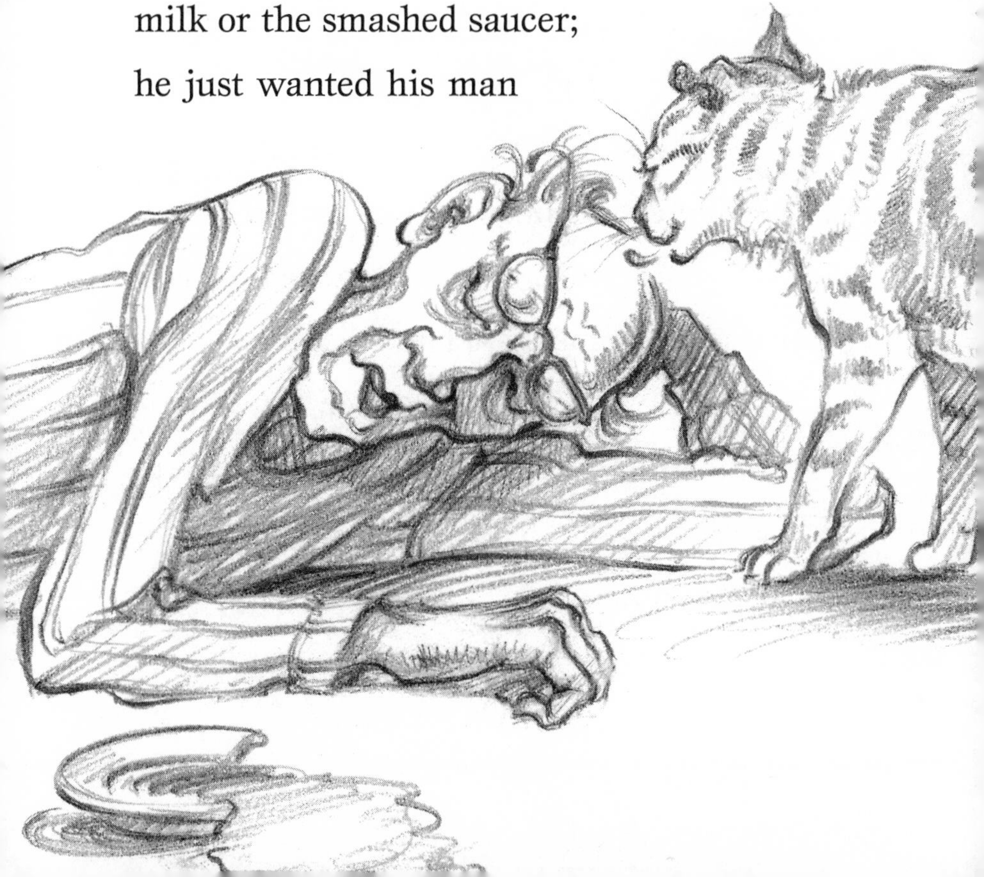

to wake up. He licked Mr. Larsen's face, nudged his hands, and yowled in his ear, over and over, until finally the old man began to wake up.

Mr. Larsen tried to sit up and fell back down—but Buster kept on licking his face with his raspy sandpaper tongue until Mr. Larsen was ready to try again.

Slowly, slowly, with Buster nudging and yowling every time he went back to sleep, Mr. Larsen woke up enough to get his cell phone out of his pocket and dial 9-1-1.

Even when the ambulance came with its sirens and lights, Buster sat by his owner's head glaring at the men rushing into his house.

"It's okay, Buster," Mr. Larsen whispered.

Buster meowed with his ears flat and worried. He didn't think it looked okay at all.

"He saved my life," Mr. Larsen told the ambulance men as they lifted him onto a stretcher.

"Good kitty," said one of the men, and before they wheeled Mr. Larsen out of the house, they shut Buster into the living room to keep him safe.

Buster paced around the empty room, yowling as if his heart would break.

The next day there was a story in the local newspaper.

CAT SAVES OWNER'S LIFE!

Eighteen months ago, Mr. Edgar Larsen rescued a cat from the Rainbow Street Animal Shelter.

Last night, the cat returned the favor by rescuing his elderly owner.

Mr. Larsen, aged 89, fell in his kitchen, breaking his hip and losing consciousness.

Our reporters interviewed Mr. Larsen from his hospital bed. "Buster wasn't going to let me die," Mr. Larsen said. "He licked my nose and yowled in my ears till I woke up enough to call 9-1-1. That cat is a hero!"

However, in a sad twist to the tale, when Mr. Larsen's son arrived from New York City, the cat was missing. He is described as a large orange tabby cat. Anyone seeing him is asked to phone the Rainbow Street Animal Shelter.

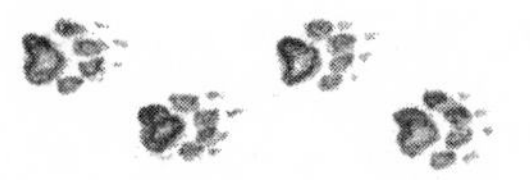

Normally Buster was a very smart cat. He could easily tell if a window was open or shut. He was good at figuring out whether he could fit through any sort of hole or open window.

But as he prowled the living room that terrible night of flashing lights and screaming sirens, Buster wasn't thinking. Buster was scared and desperate, and he wanted Mr. Larsen.

Most cats that were scared and desperate would have hidden behind the couch or under a chair, but Buster wasn't most cats.

He stared up at a window that Mr. Larsen often opened on hot nights.

The big orange cat leapt . . . and crashed right through the glass, landing on the lawn outside. He had one cut paw and a deep scratch across his head, but Buster didn't notice. He started to run.

He didn't know where he was going. He didn't know where Mr. Larsen had gone, and he wasn't even trying to follow the ambulance: he was just running.

When Buster finally stopped, he didn't know where he was.

6

Bunnies were Mrs. Lee's favorite pet, but she liked all sorts of animals, and she loved stories about amazing animals. She showed the family the newspaper article on Friday night.

"Buster!" said Josh. "That's the big cat who's exactly the same color Rex was!"

"Poor Mr. Larsen," said his mom. "And poor Buster."

"We've got to help find him!" said Josh.

So the next morning, when Josh and his family walked to the beach, they went past Mr. Larsen's house on the way.

Josh stared under bushes and into shadowy, cat-hidey corners. He stared through the high wire fence of the house that was being rebuilt next door.

"When did Mr. Larsen go to the hospital?" he asked his mom.

"Wednesday night," she said. "That's a long time for a cat to go hungry."

Josh thought about how he used to hold a carrot for Rex to nibble as a special treat.

He thought about how they always made sure Rex had clean water and hay so he was never thirsty or hungry.

He knew that Mr. Larsen would have looked after Buster the same way. But Mr. Larsen couldn't look after Buster now because he was in the hospital, and Josh's family didn't have Rex to look after. *It's not fair!* thought Josh.

"Let's look for Buster instead of going to the beach," he said.

"I was just going to say that!" everyone else said together.

They looked up into trees and down quiet alleys. They walked through the streets, around the block and the next block after that, but there was no sign of a giant marmalade cat.

Mrs. Lee made Josh's favorite noodles for dinner that night, but Josh could hardly swallow them. He kept wondering if Buster had found anything to eat.

He hated thinking about that wild, crazy cat being afraid, lost, and starving.

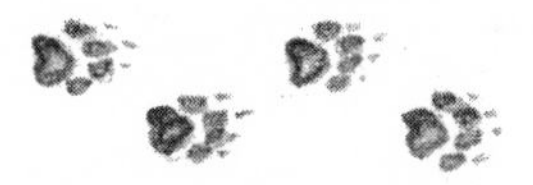

But Buster was a smart cat.

When he stopped running on that terrifying Wednesday night and realized he didn't know where he was, Buster found a quiet garden with fat bushes sprawling against the garage wall. He crawled in under the middle bush, scratched out a bed in the dirt, and curled up and slept for the rest of the night.

In the morning he sat up and groomed himself, combing the glass off his head with his claws, and licking the dried blood off his paws. His rough sandpaper tongue smoothed out the fur along his back and his tail, and then he sat on his bottom, stretching his legs and curling between them to lick his belly and everywhere else.

Buster felt calmer when he was clean. He swaggered out of his camping place as if it had always belonged to him.

The first thing he saw was a small spotty dog in the backyard on the other side of the garage. The second thing was a woman putting a bowl down on the porch and then going back inside.

Buster was ready for breakfast. He jumped to the top of the fence and over to the porch before the dog had time to see him. With a hiss and spit, Buster chased the little dog away from his bowl: dog kibble wasn't as tasty as cat kibble, but it was better than no breakfast at all.

The dog was so shocked at being chased by a cat that it quivered against the back fence for five minutes before it started to bark.

"What's the matter, Freckles?" the woman called from inside the house.

Buster munched faster.

The woman opened the door. "Get out of here!" she shouted at Buster.

Buster raced across the yard like an orange streak of lightning. He could hear the woman calling as he leapt to the top of the fence. "Come on, Freckles! That nasty cat won't get you again!"

At the end of the block, Buster stopped. He sat in the sun and groomed the dog kibble crumbs off his face and paws till he was all neat and tidy. Then, keeping close to bushes and shadowy trees, he started off in the direction he thought was home.

7

It took Buster another two days to find his way home to Mr. Larsen's house. Big dogs chased him, and people shouted at him. Cars screeched to a stop when he raced across roads without looking. He tried to steal meat from a big dog, but an even bigger dog came out from his kennel, and both dogs were so angry they jumped the fence to chase him.

That was the only time Buster was really afraid, because he could chase two little dogs or one big dog, but he couldn't fight off two big dogs. It took a long rest behind a pile of lumber and nearly ten minutes of extra grooming before he was ready to start finding his way home again after that.

But an hour later he found half a hamburger on a picnic table, and that was so good he forgot all about being afraid.

Late that night, when he'd walked as far as he wanted for one day, he sneaked in a cat door to eat a huge bowl of kibble before chasing a fluffy white cat out of its comfy bed.

"Be quiet, Bella!" a man shouted down the stairs.

The white cat slunk off to hide behind the couch while Buster snuggled into her bed. He slept happily till the first rays of morning sun shone in the window. Then he finished off the last three pieces of kibble and slipped out the cat door before anyone was awake.

Finally, early on Friday morning, he reached his home. He arched his back, rubbing happily against the front door and meowing to be let in.

When no one came to the door, Buster stalked around the house. Mr. Larsen always left the bathroom window open for him, but it was shut tight. The living room window that he'd broken had been fixed, and it was closed too. There was no way in.

Buster crept back more cautiously to the front door. He sniffed at it, and this time he didn't rub against it.

He knew that Mr. Larsen wasn't inside.

Buster felt again the terror of Mr. Larsen lying on the floor and not waking up. He remembered the flashing lights,

sirens, and people with metal trolleys taking his man away.

Buster flattened his ears and crept under a bush to wait.

A car pulled into the driveway, and Buster watched Mr. Larsen's son get out. He didn't move when Mr. Larsen's son went into the house and came out again with a can of cat food.

"Here, Buster!" Mr. Larsen's son called, waving the can as he walked around the garden. "Come on, good kitty!"

Buster heard him and saw the cat food can. He was hungry, but he didn't like Mr. Larsen's son, because whenever he visited, Buster wasn't allowed to sit near Mr. Larsen. If the men sat inside, Buster had to go out, and if the men sat on the porch, Buster was shut inside.

So he sat under the bush and waited. He waited while Mr. Larsen's son walked right past the bush Buster was hiding under. He didn't even twitch when Mr. Larsen's son sneezed right in front of him.

The problem was that Mr. Larsen's son hadn't ever spent time with cats. He thought that waving a cat food can would be enough to make a frightened cat run out to meet him with a "Thank you!" meow. Then he could go to the hospital and tell Mr. Larsen he didn't need to worry anymore.

But Buster wasn't going to go to anyone except his own Mr. Larsen.

8

Josh dreamed that he was stuck in a rabbit hole, fighting and scrabbling to get out. He wanted to scream, but he'd turned into a cat—a huge, crazy orange cat, much too big for a rabbit hole.

He woke up feeling tired and miserable. *It's not fair!* he thought. *He's not even my cat, and I still feel bad!*

But by the time he got out of bed, he knew there was only one way to stop feeling bad.

"Can we look for Buster again today?" he asked at breakfast.

"It won't be easy," said his dad. "Do you remember how good Rex was at hiding?"

Josh remembered. Two years ago, in a lightning-flashing, window-rattling thunderstorm, Rex disappeared and hid. The family searched every room, under every bed, behind the couch, and in every corner, and they'd all felt sick worrying that the bunny had somehow gotten out of the house into the stormy night.

And he remembered the birthday party feeling of seeing Rex hop into the kitchen for breakfast the next morning, as if nothing had happened.

He wanted that feeling again.

"We should check at Rainbow Street first," said his mom. "They might have found him already."

After they dropped Mai off at basketball practice, Mr. and Mrs. Lee and Josh drove to Rainbow Street.

They walked down the path toward the cherry-colored door. An old man was cleaning out a water trough, while three goats grazed under a tree. The nearest goat had only three legs.

"That poor goat!" Josh said, pointing.

The goat looked up and walked away.

"Fred doesn't like to be pointed at," said the old man. "But he does just fine with three legs now."

They went inside.

"Can I help you?" someone asked.

Josh looked around. It sounded exactly like the old man, but the only person in the room was a young woman with long dark hair wound up in a bun and a name tag that said MONA.

"You're not crazy," Mona said. "Gulliver sounds exactly like Juan."

Gulliver turned out to be a gray parrot on a perch above the desk.

"He thinks he's the receptionist," Mona added.

Josh started to laugh. It was the funniest thing he'd ever heard: a parrot who sounded like an old man and thought he was a receptionist. When Josh laughed, Gulliver laughed too. He didn't laugh like an old man. He giggled like a little girl, and that was even funnier.

Mr. and Mrs. Lee and Mona started to laugh too. It was impossible not to with the gray parrot giggling and Josh splutter-ing. He hadn't laughed since Rex had died, and now he couldn't stop. He laughed till he was gasping for breath; his stomach ached, and tears rolled down his face.

Juan came in to see what was happening.

"Hola, amigo!" said the bird, and that started Josh all over again.

"Now," said Mona, when Josh had slowed down to occasional giggles and they could all hear again, "I'm guessing you didn't come just to see Gulliver?"

"It's about Buster," said Mrs. Lee.

"The cat with attitude, we called him,"

said Mona. "I just hope that attitude is helping him survive now."

"Where do you think he'd go?" asked Josh.

"He's most likely hiding somewhere near the house or trying to get back to it," said Mona. "But a frightened animal can run a long way."

"So he could be anywhere?" asked Mr. Lee.

Mona nodded. "And wherever he is, he can't live outside on his own—we need to find him to keep him safe."

Josh felt exactly the way he'd felt when he'd thought Rex had disappeared into the thunderstorm.

9

The next day was the First Monday of the Month Assembly.

Josh left for school early. His stomach was as squirmy as if he'd swallowed a bucket of caterpillars.

He turned right at the first corner, and when he got to Mr. Larsen's house, he opened the gate.

He knocked on the door just in case someone was there. No one was. Josh walked all around the outside of the house, peering into every corner of the garden.

"Here, Buster!" he called. "Come on, kitty, kitty!"

There was no sign of a cat anywhere, not the faintest meow.

Josh walked slowly back down the path to the sidewalk. His shoulders drooped and he scuffed his feet; the caterpillars in his stomach had turned into a swarm of butterflies. He did not want to go to school.

He stared through the fence of the house that was being built next door, but the garden had been bulldozed. There were just piles of lumber and wood, metal tubes and pipes—no fat bushy shrubs for a cat to crawl under or leafy trees to climb.

Josh straightened his backpack and walked to school. The butterflies in his stomach grew into bouncing birds.

I could still change my mind, he told himself as he turned onto Ocean Street.

I don't have to do it, he thought as he waited for the crossing guard.

Why am I even thinking of doing the scariest thing I can think of doing? he wondered as he walked in the gate.

Because Buster's a lot more scared than I am, he decided as he stepped into the auditorium. But right now he felt so scared that it was hard to believe.

What Josh didn't ask himself was why it was so important for him to help Buster. That question had been spinning around at the back of his mind all night, till there wasn't even any point in wondering about it anymore.

He just knew he had to do it.

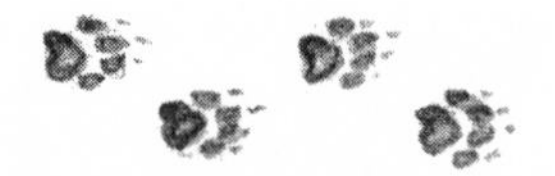

Principal Stevens talked to the kids who were presenting this morning. Hannah was the last in line; Josh could see her ponytail quivering with tension.

Josh had forgotten he hadn't wanted to listen to her talk about the animals in

Rainbow Street. Now he just wished that Buster was one of them.

He took a deep breath and marched up to the principal.

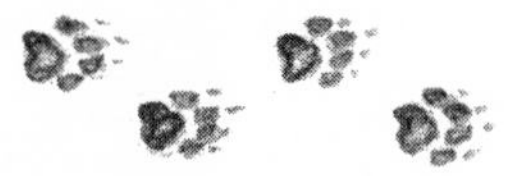

It was the longest assembly Josh had ever sat through. There were announcements from teachers and reports from class captains, two girls singing a duet, and a boy playing a violin solo. It felt like a week of detention.

Hannah was on next. She stepped up to the dais and told them about a dog who'd arrived at the shelter last week and was ready to be adopted.

"He's friendly and very, very cute," said

Hannah, showing a picture of a shaggy gray and white dog peeking out from beneath woolly bangs.

"Awww," breathed the audience. Josh hoped they'd care as much about an ugly orange cat.

Hannah finished, and Principal Stevens said, "Finally, we have one more urgent item."

Josh walked across the stage. He could hardly breathe; his throat felt as if he'd swallowed a baseball. His stomach was sick of the jiggling caterpillars, butterflies, and birds and was ready to throw up.

He really, really didn't want to throw up onstage.

The microphone was too tall; he was a lot shorter than Hannah. He heard someone laughing as he struggled to bend it down.

You can't run away now! Josh told himself.

He held up the poster he'd printed, with a picture he'd found online of a big orange

cat. The screen behind him blew it up to a giant size so that even the kids in the very back row could see it.

"Except Buster's got one bent ear," said Josh. "And enormous paws."

His voice squeaked as he said "enormous." The microphone caught the squeak and the word echoed shrilly through the auditorium.

"To catch squeaky mice?" said a boy in the front.

"For a pipsqueak!" said someone else, and a wave of laughter rippled through the 780 kids, building from kindergartner giggles to loud bully laughs.

Principal Stevens stepped forward.

"That'll do!" she snapped. "Josh has something serious to tell us."

Josh moved quickly to the headline from the newspaper article: *Cat Saves Owner's Life!*

Finally, phone numbers for the Lees and the Rainbow Street Shelter flashed on the screen. "These numbers are on the poster I'm putting up on the bulletin board too," Josh finished desperately. "Buster's not an ordinary cat. He's a hero. So if you think you've seen him, please tell me or take him to the shelter."

His knees were wobbling as he walked across the stage to the other presenters. Hannah smiled.

"You're not going to throw up, are you?" she whispered.

Josh's face glowed red as a traffic light. "How did you know?"

"How do you think?" she asked. "It's the fourth time I've stood up there."

Josh stared in surprise.

"Don't look so worried!" Hannah laughed. "The good news is I haven't thrown up yet."

"Anyway," Josh muttered, "it's the last time I'm doing it."

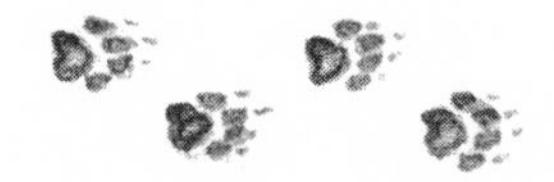

Logan, the boy who'd lost his dog at the start of the year, caught up to him as they crowded into their classroom.

"That was great," Logan said. "I'd never have thought of presenting it at assembly when I lost Bear. I really hope you find Buster."

"Me too," said Josh.

All the rest of the day, some kids made squeaky-mouse noises when they saw him. But others came up and said that they had a cat too or they had a pet who'd gotten lost once, and that they'd look for Buster on their way home. Even kids who didn't have a pet stopped and said, "I hope you find your cat."

Josh's head swirled with the muddle of feelings: hot shame about his squeaky voice, squirmy embarrassment when kids thought Buster was *his* cat, warm squishy feelings from the kids who cared—and over it all, the cold fear that Buster was lost forever.

Because even the next day, even after some kids had said they'd looked for him on the way home from school or going to a friend's place, no one had seen a cat who could possibly be Buster.

10

After school on Tuesday, Josh and his mom went back to the Rainbow Street Shelter—but Buster hadn't turned up there either.

"We can try putting a cage trap at his house," said Mona. "I phoned Mr. Larsen's son, and he said that would be okay."

"Won't Buster hate being trapped?" Josh asked.

"Probably," said Mona. "The poor little guy's been through plenty already. But a night in a cage is better than being hit by a car."

Josh felt cold right through. It was bad enough thinking about Buster yowling in a cage, but now he couldn't stop seeing an even more horrible picture.

He had to find him!

Josh and his mom carried the cage out to the car, went back to their house for a can of tuna and an old beach towel, and drove around to Mr. Larsen's house. Josh felt like a burglar, sneaking up to someone's porch knowing he wasn't home.

"We're doing the right thing," his mom said, but she knocked on the door first, just like Josh had the morning before. Just like when Josh did it, there was no answer.

They opened the can of tuna and walked all around the garden again, brushing branches aside and peering into corners. "Here, Buster!" they called. "Kitty, kitty, kitty!"

They walked more slowly and crept into more cat-hidey corners than Mr. Larsen's son had, but they still didn't see even a shadow of a cat or hear an echo of a meow.

Finally Mrs. Lee said, "We have to give up now. There's nothing more we can do."

"I'll just look here first!" said Josh,

because there was one big, fat bush that he hadn't checked. He was so sure Buster would be there that he could almost feel the cat's fur under his hands.

But Buster wasn't there either.

Josh thought about what Mona had said and helped his mom put the cage on the porch where Buster used to sit with Mr. Larsen. Josh half crawled in to spread the beach towel out, smooth and comfy for Buster to lie on. Then they put the open can of tuna inside.

Once Buster went in to eat it, the door would close so that he'd be safe till morning.

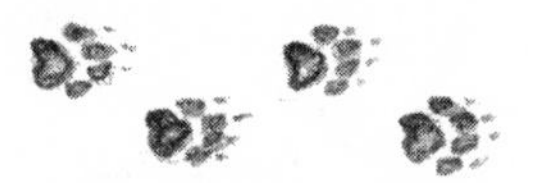

Josh woke up in the middle of the night, fighting to get out of a tangle of sheets. His heart was thumping with fear.

He lay still in the darkness for a long time, wondering whether Buster had found the can of tuna.

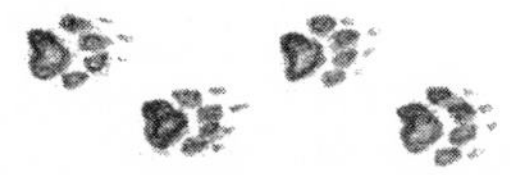

All the while that Mrs. Lee and Josh had been walking around the garden, Buster had lain flat under a bush so low to the ground it didn't look as if an enormous cat could possibly squish under it. He had smelled the tuna, but after two days of being chased and afraid, he was not going to come out for anyone.

But when they'd left, he could still smell the fish. All evening its scent wafted through the garden like a song calling his name. As soon as it was dark, Buster crept toward it.

He stretched one enormous paw into the cage, as far as he could, and batted the can. It rolled a little bit closer. Buster wanted that tuna very badly. He whacked the can harder.

It bounced against the cage wall and rolled to the other end.

No matter what Buster did, he could not get it out. And no matter how badly he wanted it, he would not walk into that cage.

Buster licked the taste of tuna off his claws and stalked into the night.

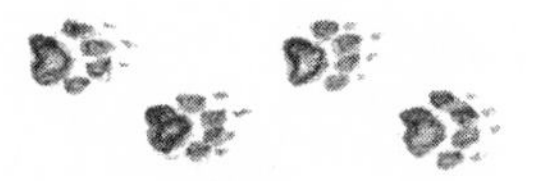

So when Mrs. Lee and Josh walked around to Mr. Larsen's the next morning, the tuna can was upside down at the end of the cage, the towel was scruffed up at the front, and Buster was nowhere to be seen.

Josh knew he should want Buster to be in the cage, but he felt like dancing and shouting to see it empty. He was glad that wild, crazy cat was free.

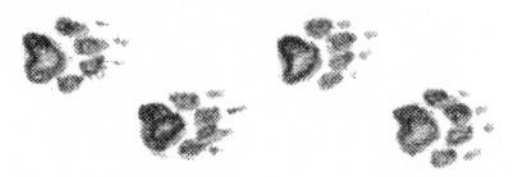

As soon as Josh and Mrs. Lee had gone, Buster came out from under his favorite bush. He slipped back up onto the porch.

Buster had barely eaten since he'd

gotten back to his house, and he was getting tired. It was hard work sneaking bits of food and hiding—and it was warm and peaceful on the porch in the morning sun. He curled up on Mr. Larsen's chair and fell fast asleep: so sound asleep that he didn't hear the man coming up the path.

"Hey, kitty!" the man said, and patted Buster on the head.

Buster opened his eyes and saw a man with a purple baseball cap leaning over him. With a nightmare yowl, he streaked off the porch, his ears flat against his skull, looking more like a tiny scared kitten than a giant crazy cat.

The baseball cap man liked cats, and

most cats liked him—so when he saw a cat as afraid as Buster, he knew there was something wrong.

"Here, kitty!" he called. "Kitty, kitty, kitty!"

He hunted all around the house and garden.

"There you are!" he said at last.

Buster was crouched in the corner of the fence behind the garage. His tail lashed and he hissed as the man came near.

"It's okay, kitty," the baseball cap man said. He was sure that Buster was a stray that needed help. *I'll take him to a shelter,* he thought, *and if nobody claims him, I'll keep him.*

He walked slowly up to the corner, still talking quietly—then lunged and grabbed at the frightened cat.

Buster flew straight up the tall fence and over the other side, disappearing into the piles of lumber and aluminum at the building site next door.

The baseball cap man shrugged, and went back to his job of hammering a big sign onto Mr. Larsen's front lawn.

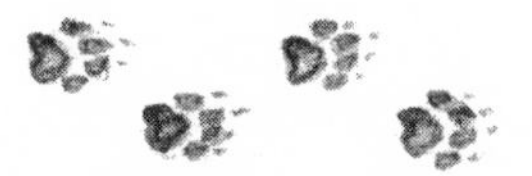

What if Buster's not hiding in his own garden? Josh thought as he walked home from school. *He might have run miles away!*

He stared through the fence at the construction site. It didn't look like a place for a cat to hide, but he liked seeing what was happening.

Nothing had changed today: no more walls were up, and the big aluminum pipes were stacked where they'd been this morning.

Then Josh heard something.

"Meow."

It was very faint. It sounded far away, and it didn't sound tough enough to be a giant cat with attitude.

"Buster?" Josh called, walking back and forth beside the fence. "Buster?"

"Meow," the cat called back.

It still sounded faint, and it didn't sound happy.

Josh raced back to Mr. Larsen's garden and behind the garage. "Buster?" he called again.

He couldn't hear the meowing at all now, but there were scuff marks in the dirt and a tuft of orange cat fur on the fence. Buster had been there.

Josh dragged Mr. Larsen's chair off the porch and around to the back corner. Standing on the chair, he could pull himself up to the top of the fence.

It was higher than he'd thought, but he perched on top, one leg on either side of the fence as if he was riding a horse.

Josh swung his right leg over and jumped down into the building site. He landed on his hands and feet, brushed the dirt off his hands, and called again.

"Buster?"

The meowing started again. It was coming from the pile of aluminum pipes.

11

Josh raced over to the stack of pipes. He crawled all around them, peering into each one, but could not see a cat.

He tried to lift one, but it was much too heavy. He hoped Buster wasn't trapped under them!

Josh put his foot on the bottom pipe and tried to roll it. It rocked back and forth.

"MEOW!"

The sound was coming from deep inside the pipe.

It was the one that had a joining piece like a bent elbow, then a short pipe finishing in a grid. It sounded as if Buster had gotten himself around that bend and didn't know how to get back.

Josh wished he were so big and strong that he could just pick up the pipe and gently slide Buster down toward him. But he wasn't big and strong. He was small and skinny.

A little voice in Josh's head said he should go home and get help, but Josh didn't have time to listen to anyone, not even his own brain.

He wiggled into the pipe after the cat.

It was like crawling through the playground tunnel when he was in kindergarten, except that it was a lot narrower. The kindergarten tunnel had been wide enough for little kids to crawl through on their hands and knees; Josh could probably still have done it now.

This pipe wasn't wide enough to get up on his hands and knees. There wasn't even room for his elbows to spread out to the side to pull him along: the only way was to wiggle like a snake. His T-shirt rumpled up around his chest; the metal ridges pressed cold and hard against his stomach.

It was a lot darker than the playground tunnel too, because it was made of metal and wasn't open at the other end.

But the main difference was that this one had a giant terrified cat stuck around the bend.

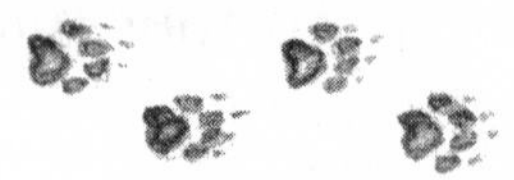

Josh was at the joint. Now that he'd nearly reached Buster, he remembered all the things he should have thought of first, like a cat-tempting can of tuna or a towel to wrap him in.

Josh wiggled his head and shoulders around the bend. He could just see the cat's shape as Buster backed up, flattening himself against the grid.

"Hi, Buster," said Josh. "It's me."

Buster meowed. It was the little-kitten meow that Josh had heard from the outside. He hated to hear that big crazy cat so helpless.

"It's okay," Josh told him. "I'm going to get you out of here."

Very, very slowly, he reached toward the cat. "Mr. Larsen wouldn't like you to be stuck in here, would he?" he asked. He knew that Buster didn't understand what he was saying, but he had to keep on trying. "Mr. Larsen says you're a hero. He wants you to come out and have a nice can of tuna."

Buster pushed his head against Josh's hand and let Josh stroke gently over his head and down his neck, which was as far as he could reach.

"You ready to go back now?" Josh asked.

Buster didn't move.

Josh wiggled a bit farther. Now he could reach right around the cat, but he kept his face down against the metal floor. If he was going to get scratched, the back of his head was better than his face.

"This is probably the dumbest thing I've ever done," he told Buster.

With his arm around the cat's back, he pulled Buster gently toward him. Buster didn't scratch or fight, but he didn't help either; he just let Josh pull him, as if he was too tired to care what happened.

It's not easy wiggling backward around a bend in a tight metal tunnel, but it's even harder when you're pulling a cat who doesn't want to move. For a minute Josh thought he wasn't going to be able to do it. He was back in his nightmare, fighting to get out and wanting to scream—and wishing he'd gone home and asked for help instead of crawling in here all alone.

But screaming would scare Buster more. All Josh could do was wiggle slowly backward, coaxing the cat and pulling him, inch by inch.

He slid his shoulders out of the bend, then his head—and slowly, slowly, Buster backed down the tunnel toward him.

The pipe was even longer than it had been going in. Josh didn't know how long he'd been in there, and he couldn't guess how much more he had to go.

His left foot touched dirt.

Josh paused. He was nearly there—but he was going to have to hold on tight to Buster for those last few wiggles. He couldn't lose the cat just as they burst free of the tunnel!

He was concentrating so hard it took a minute to hear the voice from outside. "Josh! Josh—are you in there?"

"I've got Buster," he called. "He's really scared."

"So was I!" snapped his mom.

Josh stood up with Buster in his arms. His mom's face looked tense. Behind her were two construction workers.

"When I found your bag behind the fence, I phoned the number on the gate here," she said. "These men came and let me in."

"There's a reason it's locked," the taller man said. "We don't want kids getting hurt going places they're not supposed to be."

"Sorry," said Josh.

"Lucky you're so skinny. If you'd gotten stuck in that pipe, you'd have been in real trouble!"

Josh carried Buster to where Mrs. Lee had parked in front of Mr. Larsen's house. Buster was heavy, but Josh liked carrying him, and Buster seemed to think that was okay.

There was a sign on the front lawn. It read: FOR SALE.

12

"We'll take Buster to Rainbow Street to get checked out," said Josh's mom. "Then they'll be able to give Mr. Larsen the good news."

Mona had told them that Buster didn't like going in cars, so Mrs. Lee got the beach towel from the cage. She wrapped it around the frightened cat, then settled the Buster-in-a-blanket into Josh's arms.

And maybe it was because she drove to Rainbow Street so slowly and carefully or maybe because he knew that Josh had saved him, but Buster didn't panic at all.

Mona was waiting for them at the gate. "Hey, Hero Cat," she said softly, leaning in to stroke the furry orange head.

Buster rubbed against her hand and meowed, sounding a little more like himself and a little less like a scared kitten.

"And Hero Boy," Mona added. "I guess your mom's already told you what a dangerous thing you did—so I'll just say thanks."

She slipped a harness over Buster's shoulders, clipped on a leash, and handed it to Josh. "For most cats, we use a carrying case," she said. "But Buster is not most cats!"

Josh felt as proud as when she'd called him Hero Boy.

As if he'd understood what Mona was saying, Buster decided he'd had enough of being a cat in a blanket and jumped down to the sidewalk.

Josh and Buster walked up the path to the cherry-colored door. Buster was almost swaggering again by the time they got into the vet's examination room.

The vet checked inside Buster's mouth and ears, felt all over his body, took his temperature, and listened to his heart. "He's got a few cuts and scratches. He's hungry and tired, and still in a little bit of shock," he said. "But he's going to be absolutely fine."

"But there is a problem," Mona said, and her eyes filled with tears.

Josh held his breath. He didn't understand what else could be wrong.

"Buster's okay, but Mr. Larsen isn't," said Mona. "The doctors have told him that his hip is never going to be strong enough for him to live alone again. He's going to move in with his son."

"But his son's in New York City!" said Mrs. Lee.

"Yes," said Mona. "But the real problem

is that he's allergic to cats. Mr. Larsen can't take Buster with him."

Josh felt as if he were standing in the ocean and a strong wave had washed the sand away from under his feet. "What's Buster going to do?"

His voice squeaked worse than it had in assembly, but he didn't care.

"Mr. Larsen asked if we could find him a new home."

"No!" shouted Josh. "We can't leave him here again!"

His mom had already pulled out her phone. "Meet us at the Rainbow Street Animal Shelter," she told Mr. Lee and Mai. "It's urgent!"

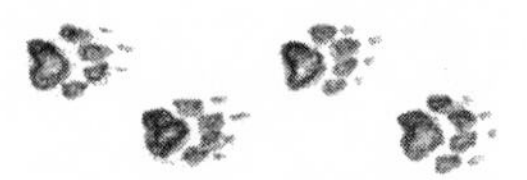

"Have you thought about this?" Mona asked when the whole family was there. "When you came in before, Mrs. Lee wanted a baby bunny, and Mr. Lee said Mai wanted a dog."

"I never wanted a pet again," admitted Josh.

"But now you're choosing a cat?" said Mona.

"Not just any cat!" they all said. "It's Buster."

Mona smiled. "Sometimes that happens," she said. "Sometimes life chooses a pet for you."

13

At first Buster liked doing only the things that he used to do with Mr. Larsen. He liked going for a walk at the beach every afternoon and sitting on the back step when they had dinner on the patio.

Mrs. Lee bought him a ball with a bell inside, and Josh made him a sock toy filled with catnip. Buster just watched when someone tossed the jingly ball or the sock toy toward him. He looked as if he didn't even know that they were trying to play.

He never tried to run away, but one afternoon when Josh was walking him on his leash, Buster turned to go up the street past Mr. Larsen's old house.

"You don't live there anymore," Josh reminded him.

But Buster sat on the sidewalk and wouldn't move until Josh turned right. They walked up the street.

A young woman was sitting on the porch where Mr. Larsen used to sit. She was watching two toddlers playing in a new sandbox and smiled when she saw Josh and his wild crazy cat walking on a leash.

"That's the biggest cat I've ever seen!" she called. "What's his name?"

"Buster," said Josh.

Buster quivered, and started walking again.

That night, when Mrs. Lee was making dinner, she accidentally dropped a long curling carrot peel on the floor. Buster leapt and caught it, then threw and chased it all around the living room till he lost it behind the couch cushions. He couldn't get his paw down the back of the couch. He meowed loudly for someone to find it for him.

Mr. and Mrs. Lee, Mai, and Josh all came running. Mr. Lee pulled out the broken carrot peel, and Mrs. Lee peeled a new one. She tossed it onto the floor—and Buster leapt after it.

When that carrot peel was too broken to throw, Josh got out the fishing pole he'd made. He trailed the feather in front of Buster, and the big cat pounced. Josh flicked it high, and Buster leapt high. They played around and around the room, trailing and pouncing, flicking and leaping.

By the time Josh's favorite TV show

came on, Buster had shredded the feather and torn it right off the fishing pole string. Josh got a piece of paper and crumpled it into a tight ball. He sat on the couch so he could watch TV while he tied the paper ball at the end of the string.

Buster bounded across the room and poured himself onto Josh's lap. As Buster settled in, he began to purr. It started off as a whispery hum, but as the boy's hands

stroked the thick fur from the top of his head, down his back to the start of his tail, Buster's purr rumbled louder and louder. After a few minutes, his whole body thrummed and he sounded like a fishing boat heading out to sea.

Dear Josh,

Thank you very much for your letter and the pictures of Buster. Asking the folks at Rainbow Street to find Buster a new home was the hardest thing I've ever done, and it makes me very happy to know he's settled in with you.

I'm sending you a picture too, because last week my son and his wife brought home a little dog from the animal shelter here. It's mostly poodle, so my son is not allergic to it.

I didn't think I ever wanted to get to know another animal, but this little dog didn't give me a choice. Buster will always have his own space in my heart, but it seems there's room for a mostly poodle as well.

Thank you for finding space for Buster in your heart and your home.

Yours truly,

Edward Larsen

COMING SOON:

Turn the page for a sneak peek!

Sam and her parents had read all the information sheets that Mona had given them, but they still couldn't decide which animal would be the best pet.

They learned that hamsters like to sleep in the day and sometimes get grumpy if they're woken up, that gerbils are happier if there are two of them but they need to be from the same litter, and that rats can learn to do tricks.

Mrs. Ballart worried that rabbits needed too much room, and Mr. Ballart worried that the fancy mice might escape.

Sam's mind was running in circles and getting nowhere, exactly like the brown and white hamster in his wheel.

"Don't worry," said her mom when she kissed Sam goodnight. "It'll turn out okay, no matter what you choose."

Sam tried to smile, but she almost wished that she'd never asked for a pet if it was going to be this hard to choose!

But that night, she dreamed of cuddling an animal with soft, thick hair. It was small but solid and sat quietly on her lap. It wasn't any of the animals that she'd actually held at the Rainbow Street Animal Shelter.

"I want a guinea pig," Sam said when she woke up. A quiet bubble of happiness was swelling inside her, and she knew she was right.